In loving memory of Carol J. Buckley, shining star
of the Cornell University Library, who always had room
in her heart for a new friend.
We miss you.

M. K.

To Priscilla, our first personal librarian

K. H.

Text copyright © 2006 by Michelle Knudsen
Illustrations copyright © 2006 by Kevin Hawkes

First edition 2006

Library of Congress Cataloging-in-Publication Data

Knudsen, Michelle.
Library lion / Michelle Knudsen ; illustrated by Kevin Hawkes. —1st ed.
p.   cm.
Summary: A lion starts visiting the local library but runs into trouble
as he tries to both obey the rules and help his librarian friend.
ISBN-13: 978-0-7636-2262-6
ISBN-10: 0-7636-2262-1
[1. Lions—Fiction. 2. Libraries—Fiction. 3. Obedience—Fiction.]
I. Hawkes, Kevin, ill. II. Title.
PZ7.K7835Lib 2006
[E]—dc22   2006042578

2 4 6 8 10 9 7 5 3 1

Printed in China

This book was typeset in New Clarendon.
The illustrations were done in acrylic and pencil.

Candlewick Press
2067 Massachusetts Avenue
Cambridge, Massachusetts 02140

visit us at www.candlewick.com

Library Lion

MICHELLE KNUDSEN

illustrated by
KEVIN HAWKES

CANDLEWICK PRESS
CAMBRIDGE, MASSACHUSETTS

One day, a lion came to the library.
He walked right past the circulation desk
and up into the stacks.

Mr. McBee ran down the hall to the head librarian's office. "Miss Merriweather!" he called.

"No running," said Miss Merriweather, without looking up.

"But there's a lion!" said Mr. McBee. "In the library!"

"Is he breaking any rules?" asked Miss Merriweather. She was very particular about rule breaking.

"Well, no," said Mr. McBee. "Not really."

"Then leave him be."

The lion wandered all around the library. He sniffed the card catalog.

He rubbed his head against the new book collection.

Then he padded over to the story corner and went to sleep.

No one was sure what to do. There weren't any rules about lions in the library.

Soon it was time for story hour. There weren't any rules about lions at story hour, either.

The story lady seemed a little nervous. But she read out the first book's title in a good, clear voice. The lion looked up. The story lady kept reading.

The lion stayed for the next story. And the story after that. He waited for another story, but the children began to walk away.

"Story hour is over," a little girl told him. "It's time to go."

The lion looked at the children. He looked at the story lady. He looked at the closed books. Then he roared very loud.

RAAAHHRRRR!

Miss Merriweather came striding out of her office. "Who is making that noise?" she demanded.

"It's the lion," said Mr. McBee.

Miss Merriweather marched over to the lion. "If you cannot be quiet, you will have to leave," she said in a stern voice. "Those are the rules!"

The lion kept roaring. He sounded sad.

The little girl tugged on Miss Merriweather's dress. "If he promises to be quiet, can he come back for story hour tomorrow?" she asked.

The lion stopped roaring. He looked at Miss Merriweather.

Miss Merriweather looked back. Then she said, "Yes. A nice, quiet lion would certainly be allowed to come back for story hour tomorrow."

"Hooray!" said the children.

The next day, the lion came back.
"You are early," said Miss Merriweather.
"Story hour is not until three o'clock."
The lion did not budge.

"Very well," said Miss Merriweather.
"You might as well make yourself
useful." She sent him off
to dust the encyclopedias
until it was time for
story hour.

The next day, the lion came early again. This time, Miss Merriweather asked him to lick all the envelopes for the overdue notices.

Soon the lion began doing things without being asked. He dusted the encyclopedias. He licked the envelopes. He let small children stand on his back to reach books on the highest shelves.

Then he curled up in the story corner to wait for story hour to begin.

At first, the people in the library were nervous about the lion. But soon they got used to having him around. In fact, he seemed very well suited for the library. His big feet were quiet on the library floor. He made a comfy backrest for the children at story hour. And he never roared in the library anymore.

"What a helpful lion," people said. They patted his soft head as he walked by. "How did we ever get along without him?"

Mr. McBee scowled when he heard that. They had always gotten along fine before. No lions were needed! Lions, he thought, could not understand rules. They did not belong in the library.

One day, after he had dusted all the encyclopedias and licked all the envelopes and helped all the small children, the lion padded down the hall to Miss Merriweather's office to see what else there was to do. There was still some time left before story hour.

"Hello, Lion," said Miss Merriweather. "I know something you can do. You can bring a book back into the stacks for me. Let me just get it down from the shelf."

Miss Merriweather stepped up onto the step stool. The book was just out of reach.

Miss Merriweather stood on her toes. She stretched out her fingers.

"Almost . . . there . . ." she said.

Then Miss Merriweather stretched a little too far.

"Ouch," said Miss Merriweather softly. She did not get up.

"Mr. McBee!" she called after a minute. "Mr. McBee!"

But Mr. McBee was at the circulation desk. He could not hear her calling.

"Lion," said Miss Merriweather. "Please go and get Mr. McBee."

The lion ran down the hall.

"No running," Miss Merriweather called after him.

He put his big front paws up on the circulation desk and looked at Mr. McBee.

"Go away, Lion," said Mr. McBee. "I'm busy."

The lion whined. He pointed his nose down the hall toward Miss Merriweather's office.

Mr. McBee ignored him.

Finally, the lion did the only thing he could think of to do. He looked Mr. McBee right in the eye. Then he opened his mouth very wide. And he roared the loudest roar he had ever roared in his life.

RA

Mr. McBee gasped.

"You're not being quiet!" he said to the lion. "You're breaking the rules!"

Mr. McBee walked down the hall as fast as he could.

The lion did not follow him. He had broken the rules. He knew what that meant. He hung his head and walked toward the doors.

Mr. McBee did not notice. "Miss Merriweather!" he called as he walked. "Miss Merriweather! The lion broke the rules! The lion broke the rules!"

He burst into Miss Merriweather's office.

She was not in her chair.

"Miss Merriweather?" he asked.

"Sometimes," said Miss Merriweather from the floor behind her desk, "there is a good reason to break the rules. Even in the library. Now please go call a doctor. I think I've broken my arm."

Mr. McBee ran to call a doctor.

"No running!" Miss Merriweather called after him.

The next day, things were back to normal. Almost.

Miss Merriweather's left arm was in a cast. The doctor had told her not to work too hard.

"I will have my lion to help me," Miss Merriweather thought. But the lion did not come to the library that morning.

At three o'clock, Miss Merriweather walked over to the story corner. The story lady was just beginning a story for the children. The lion was not there.

People in the library kept looking up from their books and computer screens, hoping they would see a familiar furry face. But the lion did not come that day.

The lion did not come the next day, either. Or the day after that.

One evening, Mr. McBee stopped by Miss Merriweather's office on his way out. "Can I do anything for you before I go, Miss Merriweather?" he asked her.

"No, thank you," said Miss Merriweather. She was looking out the window. Her voice was very quiet. Even for the library.

Mr. McBee frowned as he walked away. He thought there probably was something he could do for Miss Merriweather, after all.

Mr. McBee left the library. But he did not go home.

He walked around the neighborhood.
He looked under cars. He looked behind bushes.

He looked in backyards and trash cans and tree houses.

Finally he circled all the way back to the library.

The lion was sitting outside, looking in through the glass doors.

"Hello, Lion," said Mr. McBee.

The lion did not turn around.

"I thought you might like to know," said Mr. McBee, "that there's a new rule at the library. No roaring allowed, unless you have a very good reason—say, if you're trying to help a friend who's been hurt, for example."

The lion's ears twitched. He turned around.

But Mr. McBee was already walking away.

The next day, Mr. McBee walked down the hall to Miss Merriweather's office.

"What is it, Mr. McBee?" asked Miss Merriweather in her new, sad, quiet voice.

"I thought you might like to know," said Mr. McBee, "that there's a lion. In the library."

Miss Merriweather jumped up from her chair and ran down the hall.

Mr. McBee smiled. "No running!" he called after her.

Miss Merriweather didn't listen.

Sometimes there was
a good reason to break the rules.
Even in the library.